D0786294

ADDIS
BERNER BEAR
FORGETS

For London and the people who
have lent it to me

www.fsgkidsbooks.com

Library of Congress Cataloging-in-Publication Data
Stewart, Joel.
    Addis Berner Bear forgets / Joel Stewart.— 1st American ed.
        p.   cm.
    Summary: A musical bear visits the city and finds the experience a bit overwhelming
until he remembers the reason for his trip.
    ISBN-13: 978-0-374-30036-4
    ISBN-10: 0-374-30036-4
    [1. City and town life—Fiction.   2. Memory—Fiction.   3. Musicians—Fiction.
4. Bears—Fiction.]   I. Title.

PZ7.S84928 Ad 2008
[E]—dc22
                                                                    2007044778

ADDIS BERNER BEAR FORGETS

JOEL STEWART

FARRAR, STRAUS AND GIROUX
NEW YORK

When Addis Berner Bear came
to the city it was winter.

It was so big and confusing,

so loud and fast,

that he forgot everything he had left behind.

But he forgot why he had come, too.

Addis found his way a little,

spoke to the people who would speak to him,

and took shelter where he could.

Time and a lot of things went by.

Some made his heart leap,

some made his fur bristle,

some made him cross-eyed.

It was all so much, and still
Addis Berner Bear couldn't remember
why he had come to the city.

He wasn't the only one.

Then something terrible happened.
Addis was robbed.

And something amazing!
A spring concert.

Addis Berner Bear remembered why he had come
to the city. He was top of the bill!

But how in the world could he play
for everyone without his trumpet?

Addis Berner Bear played.

The music was big and confusing,
loud and fast.

It was heart-leaping,

fur-bristling,

cross-eye making

. . . and beautiful.